CALUM KERR is a writer, editor, speaker, Lecturer
in Creative Writing at the University of
Portsmouth, and Founder of the UK's National
Flash Fiction Day. His work has appeared in a
number of places—online and in print—and was
featured on BBC Radio 4's *iPM* programme. He
lives in Southampton with his wife, his stepson,
his dog and two cats.

Other books by Calum Kerr
SHORT STORY COLLECTIONS
Wordsmith

FLASH-FICTION COLLECTIONS
31
Braking Distance
Lost Property
The 2014 Flash365 Anthology
Special Delivery

2014 FLASH365 COLLECTIONS
1: *Apocalypse*
2: *The Audacious Adventuress*
3: *The Grandmaster*
4: *Lunch Hour*
5: *Time*
6: *In Conversation with Bob and Jim*
7: *Saga*
8: *Strange is the New Black*
9: *The Ultimate Quest*
10: *Christmas*
11: *Graduation Day*
12: *Post Apocalypse*

NOVELS
Undead at Heart

TEXT BOOKS
The World in a Flash: How to Write Flash-Fiction
York Notes Advanced: The Kite Runner
York Notes AS & A2: The Kite Runner

The Girl in his Home

Calum Kerr

Published by Gumbo Press

First Published 2020 by Gumbo Press.
Printed via KDP

Gumbo Press
18 Caxton Avenue
Bitterne
Southampton
SO19 5LJ
www.gumbopress.co.uk

A CIP Catalogue record for this book
is available from the British Library

ISBN 9798656386272

There's no place like home.

'Home is the place where,
when you have to go there,
They have to take you in.'
                    - 'The Death of the Hired Man'
                              by Robert Frost

'Home is where one is most emotionally
attached.'
                              - Pliny the Elder

1.

The street was deserted.

It was the middle of the day and almost everyone was at work or school. The rest were sheltering from the thin drizzle that was blurring the outlines of the houses and cars.

Toby scanned around him as he walked. He paused outside the row of abandoned shops, looking at the boards on the windows, and the For Let signs. The letters had been taken down from the wall of the pub, but the words *Horse and Hounds* could still be read in shadows on the bricks.

He shook his head and continued on his way.

At number ninety-seven he turned up the path and walked around and down the side of the house. There was no car on the driveway and the windows were locked tight.

The back lawn was in need of a mow, but otherwise it all looked much as he remembered it. He gazed around for a few moments, letting recollections run through him, then he turned to the house itself.

The patio doors were exactly where they had always been, though these looked newer than the slightly rusted, metal ones of his childhood.

It didn't matter. Despite their corrosion-free whiteness, they wouldn't pose much of a challenge.

He pulled a screwdriver from his pocket and stepped up to them. He slid it along the track at the bottom and then, at just the right point, pushed it inwards. There was a crack and a groan, and the door separated from its track. He levered it the rest of the way up, and felt it start to slide. He gave the glass a bump with his shoulder and the door slipped back onto its tracks, now free of its lock.

He straightened up, pushed it the rest of the way open, and stepped in.

This had been the dining room, way back when, but was now being used as a kind of conservatory, with white-upholstered chairs arranged facing out into the garden, and a wicker coffee table in their midst.

He pulled the door shut behind him, and then walked on tip-toe through to the doorway that led to the hall. He paused on the threshold and listened. It was the middle of the day and the house seemed empty, but there was no sense taking chances. He stood with his head cocked to the side, his mouth wide open to quiet his breathing. He waited and waited, but there was nothing except the ticking of a clock somewhere deeper in the house.

Although now sure the house was empty, he stayed where he was. As the minutes ticked onwards, he stood with his toes on the metal strip that separated him from the rest of the house. It seemed impossible to move. He tried to convince himself that this was being caused by the reason he was here, but he knew it was something else.

It was the house.

He hadn't been prepared for the effect it would have on him.

It had always been his plan to come here, but he hadn't expected the flood of memories that it brought, so he stood in the safety of this room, and tried to force himself to take the next step.

He wasn't sure if it was fear that the rest of the house would, like this room, be different, or whether it might not have changed enough. Maybe it would be just as he remembered, or at least close enough. Would he still be able to do what he was here for if it was still the same place?

He rocked back and forth on his heels. He wanted to do it in this house, but the reality of it had the potential to be too much.

For a moment he imagined his mum walking out of the kitchen and spotting him in the doorway to the dining room, and he almost bolted.

But the moment of panic subsided. He took several deep breaths and steeled himself, and then he stepped out into the hallway.

He hurried down, past the kitchen, and turned right, mounting the open-sided stairs which formed the back of the lounge. He didn't look around as he walked, but was aware that while the basic layout of the house was no different, it had been redecorated and the furniture was new and arranged in unfamiliar places. The differences were enough to settle his mind, so when he reached the top of the stairs he was able to turn left and walk into the bedroom without a pause.

This room was arranged exactly as he remembered, but with fitted wardrobes and a sloping ceiling forming constraints to originality, there were few other options. However, the wallpaper was new, and all of the furniture and bedding were unfamiliar.

It was enough.

Toby wandered to the window and looked out. The view was the same as it ever was, but he was looking at it from a much higher angle now. In his memory he was peering over the windowsill, his hands gripping onto the gloss-painted wood, and his feet pushing him up onto his tiptoes. Now, he was tall enough to look down on the street, but even so it looked just as he remembered.

In the end, he told himself, it was right. Despite his qualms, this was the place he needed to be.

With his resolution screwed in place, Toby walked back to the bed and perched on the end.

He remembered sitting here, talking with his parents, discussing the day ahead or the day just gone. He remembered opening Christmas presents on this bed, being brought here for comfort after a nightmare, and sneaking in here on early mornings for some warmth and hugs.

He nodded to himself, then reached into his pocket and pulled out the pistol.

He checked it, once again, to make sure it was loaded and ready, and then he opened his mouth and slid the barrel between his teeth.

2.

The barrel of the gun felt larger in his mouth than it had looked in his hands. And colder.

The sight on the front snagged on the roof of Toby's mouth, and he jerked his head back. It snagged again, on his teeth, with a click that he heard through the bones of his skull, and his tongue came up involuntarily to lick around the hole at the end. He could taste sour oil and burning and it made him gag.

He pulled the gun all the way out of his mouth as his throat clenched, then his lips parted again to emit a moan, and he let his head fall forward as he started to cry.

They weren't hard sobs, his body didn't shake and jerk, he just cried and the tears fell. He could feel them falling onto his hands as they cradled the gun in his lap.

This wasn't a fit, it wasn't a dam bursting. This was just another bout of tears in a long line of them. A long line which had brought him all the way back to this bedroom and this bed.

He let it run his course, and as his vision

cleared he found himself staring down at the gun. He was realising that this wasn't at all as he'd imagined it. He'd thought that he would come here, it would feel like the right place, he would put the gun in his mouth and it would all be over.

But this was *hard*.

He looked at the gun. He turned it over and over in his hands and traced the edges of the trigger with his fingers, ran them around the chambers holding the bullets, the hammer, the grips, the barrel, and he wondered if he was actually going to be able to do this.

"Are you going to kill yourself?" came a voice from the doorway, and Toby shrieked in fright, dropped the gun which landed with a thump on the carpet. He pushed himself backwards on the bed.

The girl was standing just inside the room. She was somewhere over five feet tall, with short auburn hair, blue eyes and a half smile. She was wearing tight black jeans, a dark t-shirt with some kind of logo on it, and a thin black leather jacket. She looked to Toby as though she might be seventeen or eighteen, but he realised that probably meant she was no more than thirteen or fourteen. If she had been the age she looked, she'd have looked older, mid-twenties or something.

He realised his brain was racing in shock at the

girl's sudden appearance – babbling internally – and he sat up and took several deep breaths to try and calm himself and think of something to say; some way to explain.

"You know, just with the sitting on the bed, the crying, the gun. It looked like you were going to top yourself. Were you? Is that a real gun?"

The girl didn't wait for a reply. She walked into the room and stooped to pick up the pistol.

This brought Toby back to himself, and he lunged forward to grab it before she could, pulling it out from under her reaching hand.

She recoiled. "Jesus. No need to snatch. I was just going to look."

"It's not a toy," Toby said, and winced at his tone of voice.

The girl stepped back and leaned against the doors of the fitted wardrobe. "Well, duh. I guessed that. I mean, you're not going to break in somewhere, get all weepy and wail-y, and then try and blow your head off with a water pistol, are you?"

"No. But, well, if you want to look you can do it from there. You look with your eyes, not your fingers."

"You sound just like my mum," she said. "Don't touch. Look with your eyes. Don't run with scissors. Don't touch it, it might be hot. Make sure you look before you cr–" She stopped talking and clamped her lips together. She stepped towards the doorway, her hands rising into the air.

Toby was confused for a moment, then followed her gaze and realised he was pointing the gun at her. He lowered it, and took his finger away from the trigger. "Sorry," he said, and shrugged.

She let her hands fall and stared at him for a moment, then she leaned on the doorframe again.

"So, were you?"

"What?"

"Going to do it? Going to kill yourself?"

Toby looked down at the gun and back up at her.

"I… well... Look. Who are you?"

"Me, I'm Keira. I live here. Who are you?"

"I'm Toby."

She nodded as though this explained everything. "Okay, Toby. Pleased to meet you and all that shit. Now, want to tell me why you're here and planning to splash your brains all over my mum's bed? I mean, wanting to kill yourself I can understand – normal, innit? – but why here? Bit random."

Toby opened his mouth to respond, but Keira was still talking. She had straightened up and was bouncing on her toes in excitement. "Wait, don't tell me. I'll guess."

She lifted her hand to her face and stroked her chin with one finger in a classic 'thinking' motion.

16

"Now, let me look at you." She took a step into the room and fixed him with a serious expression. "From the look of you I'd say you were about forty." Toby opened his mouth to protest, but she held up her hand to quiet him. "Not till I'm done. I've seen this on Sherlock. Always wanted to try it.

"So, about forty. A little overweight. No ring on your finger, so not married. No mask, so not planning on being seen – which is also why you came in the day when you thought everyone would be out. Dark clothes, but not shifty black, so if you're a burglar you're not stupid or cliché or whatever, cos black's only for night.

"I saw you walk round the back of the house, cool as you like, and when I came in the front – with my *key*," she flashed him a smile, "I couldn't see where you had come in. So you've done this before – breaking into someone's house. With that, and your clothes, I suspect you have experience of being a burglar. Your flab suggests you don't do this very often or maybe you haven't done it for a while – cos you wouldn't be able to leg it over fences or anything, would you, not with that belly? – but you know what you're doing.

"Hmmm…" She tapped her finger on her chin, looking him up and down.

Toby, who had attempted to interrupt a number of times, but finally given in and just listened, now raised his eyebrows and gave her a half-smile.

"Well?" he asked.

She stared at him for a moment, then around the room, and then back at him. She nodded and let her hand drop to her side.

"Okay. Here's what I reckon. You used to be a burglar, when you were younger – that's how you know what you're doing. You've had a job, though, for a few years, working at a desk – which is why you're a bit flabby – but you got sacked or downsized or something and now you're all poor. You got a tip off that this place was full of, like, cash or jewels or something, and you thought you'd give it all another go. You know you can't run and jump and stuff, so you came in the day when no-one's in. When you did get in here, you looked around and realised that this was not going to be a rich place to knock off, and you got all depressed about your life and decided to end it all, using the gun you brought with you in case someone caught you and you know you can't run because of all the burgers you've eaten. And you chose my mum's bed because..."

Toby was smiling now, despite himself. He rolled his hands in a 'go on' motion.

"...Because it looked *comfy*?" She screwed her face up, almost in pain, on the last word, her voice suggesting she was less than sure of herself. She thought for a moment, then shook her head. "No. You chose it because, of all the rooms in the house, this one has the shittest wallpaper, so you thought it wouldn't be so bad if you covered it with your brains and goo!"

She spread her arms in triumph as she rounded off her deductions.

"There!" she said. "How did I do?"

Toby smiled at her and shook his head. "Almost entirely wrong," he said, and felt a little cruel when her face fell.

Then he placed a hand on his belly and pinched a roll of fat. "Apart from this, and my job, of course."

"Ha! I knew it! Just called me Keirlock Holmes!" She gave him a grin and then, before he could do or say anything, she flopped down onto the bed next to him.

"So, go on then," she prompted.

He turned to look at her. "What? This?" He held up the gun, a puzzled look on his face. "You want to watch me –"

"Ew, God no. Gross! No, tell me the real story. Tell me why you're here and all that shit. It's gotta be better than doing my homework."

Toby looked at her then back down at the gun. He slipped it back into his pocket, and took a deep breath.

3.

There's something else you were right about. I came in the day because I didn't want there to be anyone here, anyone to disturb me. As for the rest, you're lacking a key piece of information which would let everything make sense.

I came in these clothes because, well, they're my clothes. I didn't think about the colour or style. Didn't realise I looked badass enough to look like a burglar.

And yes, I know that someone of my age – only thirty-two, by the way, not forty – saying 'badass' is just embarrassing, but after you finding me here like this I guess I no longer have an embarrass-ment gland.

You see, without this one fact, you can't guess the rest. I didn't come here to burgle the place. I'm not and never have been a burglar. I didn't have a tip about cash or jewels, and I didn't know how to get in here because of experience. Well, not that kind of experience.

The fact – the key fact that you were missing – is that I was born in this house.

I came here because it's the place where I was happiest. I was able to get inside because while the doors are new, the frame isn't, and I used to make it jump its tracks all the time when I was a kid.

And I picked this bed because… well, it was my mum's bed too and I when I decided to do what I… have decided to do, it seemed like the right place.

I know the bed has changed, but it's in the same position, in the same room, in the same house. So as far as I'm concerned, this is the bed I was born in. Isn't it right that it's the bed I should die in?

***

Sorry. I didn't mean to cry. I know it's even more embarrassing than saying 'badass' but I think it's the first time I've actually said those words out-loud.

It's strange being back here, actually. I knew that my plan was to 'come home' but I didn't realise how many memories it would stir.

I was looking out the window not long before you appeared, and it all looks the same. I imagine there are new people living in all of the houses, but apart from a lick of paint here and there, it hasn't really changed.

I remember riding my bike up and down the

pavements. I remember going around, knocking on doors, asking for people to sponsor me for how many items I could fit in a matchbox. Don't ask me why. It was for school or something. Or Cubs.

No, wait, I wasn't in the Cubs, I don't think.

School, then.

I remember making friends with the other kids who lived around here and going round to their houses to play. I remember birthday parties in the back garden and Christmas snow and a whole bunch of what have to be false memories.

It always seemed to be sunny when we lived here – at least that's how I remember it. Apart from the days of kneeling on the back of the sofa in the lounge, and staring out at thunderstorms, that is.

Sun or storm, that was how it was when we lived here.

Apart from the year it snowed.

And I remember that my mum and dad loved each other, and loved me, and we were always happy.

Stupid, isn't it?

I know that's not how things were. For every sunny day I remember, or every storm, there must have been fifty grey skies, fifty drizzles, fifty nothing days. But they don't stay in your head, do they? They just pass through on their way somewhere else, and leave nothing behind.

For every time I fell asleep on the sofa and was carried up to bed, there must have been fifty rude awakenings and a slap on the bum to send me up the stairs. For every pleasant family dinner around the kitchen table, there must have been fifty cold silences or hot arguments.

For every time I felt loved, and could see that same love shining between my mum and my dad, there must have been fifty, a hundred, five hundred times when that love was absent.

Otherwise why would he have left? Why would we have had to move? Why did it all have to stop?

But, you see, I don't remember any of that. I remember being happy here. I remember not wanting to leave. I remember moving to the flat and it just being Mum. I remember asking where Dad was, where Dad was, where Dad was, and never really getting an answer.

And after that? Well, after that just led me here.

So, that's why I came here. That's why this seemed like the right place to come when I wanted to … do what I'm going to do. And that's the information you didn't have.

4.

"Blimey, you don't half talk, don't you?" Keira said, eventually.

Toby gave a lop-sided smile and nodded. "Sorry, I guess I've been thinking about it a lot. Waiting for someone to ask, if you like. But no-one has."

While Toby had been talking, Keira had moved to sit on the padded lid of the bedding box which sat against the wall by the door. She kicked her heels against the wood.

"So how old were you when you left? When you moved out?"

Toby thought for a moment. "Ten, nearly eleven, I think. It was just before my last year of junior school. I had to shift schools. It was hard."

Keira nodded. "So, if you're thirty-two, that means you moved away from here, what, twenty-one, twenty-two years ago?"

"Yeah, guess so. About that."

Keira held up a finger in a 'Eureka!' gesture. "In which case, you were the people who lived here before my mum and dad bought it?"

"What? Really?"

"Yep. I'm thirteen and my sister is seventeen, and they bought it after they got married and that was a couple of years before she was born. So, unless someone had it for, like, six months or a year, and then thought 'nah, crap, let's move' then they must have bought it from you guys."

Toby didn't say anything in response. He just let this new piece of information soak into his brain. It had already felt weird to be here but now, this new fact, this tenuous, but real connection to the person he was talking to, just made it feel all the stranger.

Keira was looking at him, almost evaluating him, and he could see that she was having a similar experience.

Then she asked, "When was this house built? Do you know?"

"I don't think it's that old. They were still building parts of the estate when I was growing up. You know the pub up the road?"

"What, the one without the roof? The Horny Hound or something?"

Toby smiled, remembering that that had been his and his friends' name for the pub too. It seemed some things didn't change. "That's the one," he said. "Well, I remember that being built."

Keira looked mock-impressed. "See," she said, "I said you was dead old."

She laughed, and to his surprise, Toby found himself laughing with her.

Then Keira stopped and Toby could see a thought crossing her face. "Hang on," she said. "So if they were still building and all that. Did your parents get this place when it was new?"

Toby shrugged, he'd never really given it much thought. "I suppose so. It can't have been very old. I mean, it looks like the houses I remember them building – same style. So, yeah, they probably got it when it was new."

"Cool!" Keira leapt up from her seat on the linen box, and did a little jig of excitement. "You know what that means, don't you?"

Toby shook his head.

"It means that you and me are the only kids to live here. That means that…" She tailed off. Her eyes widening. "Wait here!" she cried, and ran from the room.

5.

Keira ran along the landing to her room, ran inside, and stopped.

She knew what she was looking for, and where it was, but she just needed a moment to herself first. She was, if she was honest, kinda freaked out about finding the man – Toby – in the house. She'd bunked off school and had been planning to spend some time with her Xbox, but then she'd seen him creeping in. She'd followed once she was sure he'd be upstairs, then she'd crept up after him and, as she got near the top, she'd heard the crying.

Then she'd seen the man. And the gun.

She'd never seen a real gun in real life before, but she was fairly sure that was one. She had watched the man for a while, and worked out why he was there. If he was planning a robbery he wouldn't have his gun out – not with no-one in the house – and if he was planning something worse – murder or kidnapping or something – he wouldn't be crying. She might not get the best marks in school, but she wasn't stupid.

She'd thought about slipping away again, and leaving him to it, but that hadn't seemed like the right thing to do, so she'd decided to be cool. That was one thing she always did her best to get top marks in.

And it turned out that Toby was pretty cool himself. Interesting, anyway, in a way. That didn't mean she wasn't allowed to be at least a little freaked out, though. So she took a moment, in the privacy of her room, to take some deep breaths and shake out the nerves that were thrumming through her. She walked up and down the room a couple of times until she felt calm again; until she felt cool, and then she went over to the old toy box in the corner.

Mum had wanted her to throw it out, along with all the old and broken things that she stored inside it, but Keira had refused. This was her time capsule, and had been ever since ever. When she was old – like thirty or whatever – she would be able to open this and still see all the things that had ever meant something to her and remember them. These weren't just broken old toys and junk, not like Mum had said. These were souvenirs of a life.

She opened the lid and started rummaging. She knew what she was looking for – a small purple tin with the drawing of a soldier on the lid – and she found it towards the bottom of the chest.

She pulled the tin free and lifted the lid to check it contained what she thought. It did, and she grinned to herself. Toby wouldn't be expecting *this*!

She put the lid back on and stood up.

At the doorway to her room she paused to take a deep breath, and then she walked back along the short landing to her mum's room, carrying the tin with care as though it was one of those fancy Russian eggs perched on a velvet cushion.

She walked into the bedroom. Toby was still sitting on the end of the bed. She made a show of processing across the floor while he watched her. When she reached him she lowered herself to one knee, bowed her head, and stretched her arms out.

"For you, My Lord" she said.

6.

When Keira had run from the room, Toby hadn't moved. He had stared at the doorway and listened to her footsteps. He imagined the room she was heading for, picturing it in his mind as it had been back when it was his bedroom.

While she was gone he considered, for a brief moment, taking the gun from his pocket and completing his journey. But there was no way he wanted her to come back in and find him in that state.

Never mind the girl finding him, how could he have thought it would be okay for anyone to find him? How could he do that to someone?

Was this really the first time he had thought about 'after'? Had he been so wrapped up in his own misery, in the plan and its – ha – execution, that he hadn't thought what it would be like for someone to come home and find a stranger, dead, on their bed, with his blood and brains all over the place? What kind of man had he become?

He could feel a tide of panic rising inside him,

and he surged to his feet. He needed to leave. He needed to get out of this house, right now, and as far away as possible. He needed to get rid of the gun, and he needed to sort his life out, and he needed to...

He heard the sound of the girl coming back and he looked around him, considered jumping from the window, and then sat back down and waited. It was too late now. He was here.

She walked back into the room, carrying an old, battered Quality Street tin, holding it like a precious object, and paced forwards. Then she knelt and bowed, holding it out, presenting it to him.

"For you, My Lord" she said.

He took the tin from her and for one panicky moment wondered if there might be a bomb inside. Then he shook his head, trying to disperse the craziness of the thought, and prised open the lid.

Inside, lying on a bed of crumpled Christmas paper, was a small plastic crown. He reached in and took it out. Keira had lifted her head and was looking up at him.

The crown was a dull grey and the small balls which adorned the twelve points around the top were painted bronze. It was dusty and specked with dirt, and it was vaguely familiar.

He put the tin down on the bed next to him

and turned the crown around in his hands, examining it.

It was an unremarkable toy. Designed for a child's head, it was too small to fit him now, but yet he had an urge to put it on.

He looked from the crown to the girl, and back again, and then it hit him. This was his. Or, at least, it had been.

He remembered now. It had come with a sword made from the same cheap, grey plastic, with the hilt painted in the same dull bronze, and he had spent hours racing around, playing knights, engaging in imaginary sword fights and slaying imaginary dragons. He remembered hanging through the railings of the open-sided staircase, swiping at imaginary enemies while his mum shouted at him to be careful. He remembered his friend, Kevin, from across the road having something similar and the summer – always summer – afternoons spent devising ever more complex tournaments.

As all of this flooded his mind he gazed at the cheap crown in something approaching awe, and felt a prickling in his eyes and a tightness in his throat.

He shifted his gaze back to Keira and he could see from the grin on her face that his reaction had not gone unnoticed.

"It is, isn't it?" she said. "It's yours."

He nodded, unsure of his ability to say anything, and looked back down at the crown. His parents had forever been telling him off for digging in the borders, burying his cars, his soldiers, all his toys. He'd liked digging them up again, that sense of mystery and discovery. He'd forgotten about the crown.

"I found it in the garden, oh, *years* ago. I was digging in a flowerbed – you know, like kids do, hoping for treasure – and I found this! I was totally made up. I wore it for ages, even though I got mud in my hair. Mum shouted at me for that. And then, when I got too big for it, I put it away. Kept it. In my treasure chest. Real, actual treasure!"

She stood up and reached out to grab the crown, but her hands stopped before she touched it. His hands had tightened on the plastic, twisting the shape a little.

"Can I?" she asked, her voice gentle.

He stared at it for a moment, and then nodded and held it out.

She turned it in her own hands, marvelling at it. "It is yours, isn't it? You buried it. Or you lost it and it got covered over. But it's yours?"

"Yes," he said, his voice thick but steadier than he had expected.

"And you played with it?"

"Yes."

"And you loved it, didn't you?"

Again, "Yes."

She twirled, holding the crown up in the air, and then placed it gently on her head. It was far too small for her, and looking comical as it perched on top of her red hair.

"I loved it too," she said, turning back to face him. "How about that? We've never even met, and we shared a toy that we both loved. I mean, what are the chances!"

She walked over and opened one of the wardrobe doors. On the reverse side was a long mirror and she admired herself in it, striking poses.

Toby watched her and tried to get his mind around what was happening. He had wanted to come back here because of all the memories and associations this place had for him, but he had never expected anything like this. Anything like this girl.

"Who are you?" he heard himself asking.

7.

Me? Who am I? I'm just me. Keira. Not named after Keira Knightly, by the way, in case you were wondering and before you ask. Everyone always thinks that I was named for her, but how could I have been. I'm thirteen years old and she wasn't even famous thirteen years ago. Or, okay, yeah, maybe she was a bit, but not enough for my mum to think 'I know, I'll name my beautiful baby girl after that chick who pretended to be the queen in that crappy Star Wars movie. Cos that was all she had really done when I was born. Did you know she did that? Yeah, she gets killed I think. I looked it up on IMDB. She'd done, like, a couple of tiny things and that Star Wars shite, and then I was born, and *then* she got famous. So, she was probably famous cos of me, not the other way around. But, yeah, anyway, not named for her; named for my gran's middle name, if you really want to know.

What else? Well, I'm thirteen years old – but I told you that, yeah? – and my hair is naturally this colour. Mum says it'll fade as I get older, turn brown, but it's not happened yet and I'm betting she's wrong. I'm betting I'm going to be ginger for the rest of my life. I think about dyeing it sometimes, but why bother? People pay to have their hair coloured to look like mine, right? So why pay to change it? Maybe I will. I dunno.

Erm. I go to school – most of the time – but it was double Maths this afternoon – yawnsville – so I decided to ditch. I was going to play on my Xbox and chat with Shelley – she's off sick at the moment. She's off sick a lot. She's my best friend. We play Call of Duty a lot – we've got a good team thing going on there. I know we probably shouldn't have it, as we're not old enough, but Mum doesn't care about that Daily Mail crap about films and video games making you want to go out and kill people. It's a load of old bollocks, she says. Having to put up with school and life and people and not having enough money would make you want to kill people. Or being a psycho. Films and video games would just give you ideas for how to do it, not make you want to do it in the first place. That's what Mum says anyway, and I reckon she's probably right about that.

She's not right about much. But that's mums for you.

Let me see… Dad's gone. He's dead. I don't talk about that, so it's just me and Mum. We get along okay, most of the time, though she doesn't like me staying up so late. I tell her it's cos I can't sleep, but she doesn't seem to listen, or understand, or whatever. Apart from that, and her awful taste in music which she forces me to listen to in the car, we're okay. She works hard, long days, so I mostly cook my own tea. Which is fine. I can burn a pizza as well as anyone. We do okay, we've got enough money that we don't go hungry and Mum says we're not about to lose the house or get the electric cut off or anything like that. We don't have posh stuff, but we're okay. We get a holiday, most years. This year we're going to Spain. Again. But it'll be okay.

I don't tell Mum but I quite like school. Apart from Maths. Mrs Spencer thinks I might have some kind of 'condition' with numbers – you know, like people who can't read because the words keep swapping themselves around and dancing on the page like tripping pixies – but I tell her it's not that, I just don't like Maths. It's hard, and boring and I'm basically lazy. That's what Mum says anyway, when she's in a bad mood over my report.

I like English, though. That's pretty good. Books and shit. I can do that. And History is just like English but with true stuff instead of made up. You know, kings and that. I like History, it's interesting to know how people died way back when. It's like Game of Thrones, with all these kings killing each other and slaughtering villages and stuff. No dragons, though, but, you know.

I quite like Games, but that's not cool so I don't tell anyone. But I can run pretty fast and I'm not bad at most things. I'll tell you a secret, though, cos it's you and you don't know any of my friends and so you'll never tell them. I pretend to be worse at sports than I actually am. I could do much better if I wanted to – which is what Mr Jones always writes on my report, actually – but if I did they might pick me for a team or get me to join a club and then I'd have to spend my evenings and my weekends running round in the rain and doing all that. I mean, I enjoy it, but I don't want to make it a way of life.

I had my tonsils out last year.

I'm a Gemini which means I'm really two people.

I'm going to write a book one day – ooh, maybe I'll write about you.

I've never broken a bone.

My favourite food is cake, any cake. Just no marzipan – yuck!

My favourite colour is blue, most days, and black on the others.

My favourite number is seventeen, just to be difficult.

My favourite animal is a cat, but Mum says we can't have one because I'm allergic.

My other favourite food is sausages.

My favourite band is Nine Inch Nails – which is probably a surprise to you because you're looking at me and thinking Rihanna or One Direction or all that X-Factor kinda crap – and you've probably never heard of them, but they are seriously cool and if you heard them you'd love them.

My favourite place is my bed.

If you're not going to use that gun to kill yourself, can I?

8.

"What?" Toby asked, awakening from her monologue.

"Can I use that gun? Kill myself? If you're not planning on using it, that is. Shame to let a good gun go to waste."

She smiled at him as she said this, a real beamer, and Toby felt for a moment as though reality had slipped sideways.

"What?" he asked again, not sure he could trust what he had heard.

"Can I use your gun," she spoke slowly and loudly, as if to an old relative, "so I can shoot myself?"

Toby shook his head, not in rejection but to try and clear it. "What? No. Why?"

"Because you're right. It's a good idea. I think it would be just the thing to do. Take the gun, up to the temple, or maybe under the chin, and pow! Turn the lights out."

Toby pressed his hand to the shape of the gun in his pocket and squeezed.

"No! Don't be stupid. I'm not going to give you the gun to kill yourself."

"Don't call me stupid."

"But it is a stupid idea. Why on earth would you want to kill yourself?"

Keira gazed at him, unblinking, and Toby found himself looking away.

"Why would I want to kill myself? Why would *you* want to kill *your*self?" Her face started to flush with anger. "You come here, to my house, out of the blue, break in, and plan on redecorating my mum's bedroom with your brains. Do I ask you why? Do I poke and pry? Do I do *anything* but be friendly to you? No." She took a step towards the bed and, although she was smaller and much lighter than Toby, he found himself moving backwards, away from her.

"I don't ask you 'why?', I just accept that this is what you want to do, and fuck, if you still wanted to, right now, I'd let you. So, why won't you do the same thing for me?" She took another step and Toby leaned still further back. "Or at least get it over with, then I can take the gun and do whatever I want with it, can't I?"

Her face was right in front of his, and Toby could see something wild in her eyes. The good natured play now seemed too frantic, too happy. It was hiding something much darker.

"No," he said. He kept his voice low and

measured, and he met her, stare for stare. "What I chose to do to myself is my business, but I won't be responsible for you. I'm going to leave now, and I won't see you again, and I want you to promise me you won't do anything silly."

He waited, and their locked stares continued until Toby could feel the desperate urge to blink finally overtake him.

He saw a smirk cross Keira's face and realised she was as aware of the competitive nature of this encounter as he was. She leaned back, away from him, and then stepped back too.

She held up her hand towards the door.

"Go on, then," she said. "I'm not stopping you."

Toby watched her for a moment, and then pushed himself to his feet. He edged around her and towards the door, glancing around to check everything.

"The only thing, though," Keira started. She was holding her mobile in her hand and, as Toby watched, she reached up, gripped the neck of her t -shirt and yanked, causing it to rip. "The only thing is that the moment you leave I'm going to ring the police. I'm going to tell them you broke in and attacked me. I'm going to tell them that while you were panting over me, with your gun poking into my head, that you told me your name was Toby and you used to live here. How long do you think it'll take them to track you down with all that and the full physical description I'm going to give?"

Toby had stopped moving as soon as he saw the phone in her hand. Now he turned and started to move back towards the bed.

"Or?" he asked.

"Or what?" she replied.

"Exactly. Or what? I leave, you ring the police, I go to jail for attacking and molesting a child, or what? I stay, you use my gun to kill yourself? That's not going to happen. I won't let it."

Keira gestured towards the bed with her phone, as a kidnapper would with a pistol, and Toby sat.

She shrugged. "That's okay. I don't want to kill myself now. That'd be dull. I just want you to stay and answer my questions."

"Questions?" Toby was confused. This day was not turning out in any way like he'd imagined. "What questions?"

Keira shrugged again. "Dunno. I'll think of something. Want a drink?"

9.

As Keira left the room she held up her mobile phone behind her head and gave it a waggle.

Toby just watched her go and tried to put a lid on the mixture of panic and horror which was filling him up.

There was something wrong with this girl, something more than just being a teenager. Or was there? He didn't have much experience of thirteen year old girls, not even from when he was a thirteen year old boy. Maybe they were all a little bit crazy, maybe even more so in the twenty-first century. He didn't know. He wasn't sure. But he felt that what had just happened was more than just a normal teenager acting out. Something else was going on here.

He tried to think through his options, but he didn't really seem to have any. If he tried to leave before she was happy to let him go, he was going to be in serious trouble. If he tried to do something to her, to make sure she wouldn't say anything, he would be in even more trouble, and anyway that just wasn't him.

He could finally go through with his plan for the

day, and take his own life. But if he did, and she decided that her own suicide was no longer 'dull' then her death would be his responsibility. Okay, so he wouldn't know anything about it – he didn't believe in an afterlife – but the thought that he would be known as some kind of paedophile-suicide-cultist was not one he wanted to entertain. Nor was simply handing over the gun and letting her do her thing.

This wasn't how it had been meant to be. He was meant to come here, feel some peace, and get it all over with at last. It wasn't meant to hurt anyone else – not like jumping off a motorway bridge or in front of a truck or a train, options he'd considered – it was just meant to be simple and… nice.

This had got far too messy.

Nevertheless, he seemed to have no option except to sit where he was told, wait for her to return with her drink, and answer her questions until she decided that he was dull too, and let him go.

Another wave of panic went through him as the thought occurred to him that, even if she did let him go, she might still go through with her threat. She didn't need any more proof than she already had.

But what could he do?

Nothing.

He just had to wait and see what happened, play along and hope for the best.

10.

Keira turned the tap to let the water run cold, and waggled her fingers in the stream.

What the actual fuck was she playing at? Really? Had she just blackmailed a suicidal man with a gun into staying in her house so she could ask him some questions? Really?

And had she nearly spilled it all out, told him everything? She didn't even know him. Why would she tell him anything when she had barely managed to tell herself?

Her heart was still racing in her chest from the confrontation and her mouth was dry and tasted weird. The cooling water on her fingers was helping though.

She grabbed a glass from the drainer, filled it, and drank it all in one. She could feel the cold water working its way down into her stomach and she shivered.

She refilled the glass and turned off the tap, but she didn't move from the sink. She stared out at the fence and the wall of the house next door, and tried to pluck up the courage to go back upstairs.

She really didn't understand what had happened to her when she was talking to him. She had been having fun – she thought they both had – and she'd been telling him all about her, and then that question had dripped from her mouth and… She had felt like Alice having stepped through the looking glass. She was suddenly on the other side of a divide which she hadn't seen coming but which separated her from everything she knew. The world was no longer as it was, and she didn't know if she could do anything to get back.

She thought about running, but what if the man stayed on and talked to her mum? He'd seemed pretty worried about her – not just about her threat, but actually about her – so maybe he'd hang around, explain, tell her mum to have her daughter locked up for her own good.

And what if she went back upstairs and Toby said, "Yeah, sure. I've thought about it and let's do it. Come on, I'll kill you and then myself and we'll go out in a blaze of glory. Yeeha!"?

Okay, he probably wouldn't say 'Yeeha!' but what if he called her bluff?

Because it had been a bluff. She was pretty sure it had been.

Hadn't it?

And what if he just decided to kill her, to silence her? What if she'd pushed him over the edge? Was that possible?

She shook her head and tried to think of anything she could do.

If she went upstairs, apologised, told him he could go and she wouldn't do or say anything, would he believe her?

She raised her wet fingers to the tear in her NIN t-shirt and worried at the edges.

There just didn't seem to be a way out. She had to go upstairs, ask some questions, and see if she could get him to trust her again; see if she could rebuild the friendship that seemed to have been being forged; see if she could get him to leave, before her mum came home, but with no worries about what he was leaving behind.

She took a sip of the water. Her hand was shaking, making the glass tremble. She took a deep breath and turned to go back upstairs.

11.

When Keira returned to her mum's bedroom, Toby was still there. She had wondered if maybe he would have sneaked out the front while she was worrying in the kitchen, or even tried to get out of the window. Silly idea, really, the drop was too far and onto paving stones.

She wasn't sure if she was relieved or not.

He had been staring down at his hands when she came in, but looked up when she walked across and sat back on the bedding box.

Neither of them said anything for a while until he finally broke the silence.

"So," he said.

She nodded. "So."

He watched her, and waited.

She looked around the room.

"Has it changed much?" she asked, eventually.

"Sorry?"

"This room, has it changed much?"

He looked around, though he had already examined the room pretty thoroughly since his arrival. Finally, he shook his head. "Not really. The ceiling was always white – I think it was woodchip before, too, maybe even the same stuff repainted – and so were the windows and the radiator. They were just normal windows then, though, not double -glazed. So they must be new."

He turned his head, describing things as he went. "Wallpaper's new. Bed's new, and the cabinets and the chest of drawers, but in the same places. Linen box's new, and the carpet. Wardrobes are the same, though. Built in."

Keira nodded and Toby looked back at her. "Is that really what you wanted to ask me? Doesn't seem worth the fuss."

Keira shrugged.

"Come on. What is you want to know? You're the one with all the power now, so you told me. So ask your questions, and I'll answer if I can."

Keira gazed at Toby for a moment, and he wondered what she was thinking. Her mind seemed to be elsewhere, worrying over other things.

And then she was back. "Okay. I want to know why. I want to understand."

"Understand what? Why what?"

She raised a hand towards him, palm out flat as though she was offering him something. "You. Here. That gun. Your plan. I want to know why. You told me some of it, but it's not enough. I want to know why."

Toby nodded. She was asking what he'd expected, but he'd wanted to be sure.

"You want my story, is that it?"

Keira nodded, and Toby realised that despite the clothes and the makeup, she now looked no more than her thirteen years, if not younger.

"Okay," he said, and began.

12.

As I said, I was born in this house. My parents moved in, lived here for a couple of years, and then I guess they had enough money coming in so they thought they could manage a kid. Maybe I was an accident and they never planned anything of the sort. Maybe my bedroom was meant to be for guests. I don't know, my mum never told me and I never asked.

Living here was fine. It was good. I grew up, got into trouble, made friends and fought with them, went to their birthday parties and did all the things you did when you were a boy in the eighties. I played out on my own a lot more than kids seem to these days. I played football in the road, and went exploring in the woods. I went to school, enjoyed bits of it, hated others. I was always crap at sports day, I remember that much.

It was all just, you know, normal. Nothing much changed, life just went on. Dad went to work, Mum did her part-time job in the cake shop, and I thought it was going to be like that forever.

And then, of course, it all came to an end.

They didn't talk to me about it. I was too young to be allowed to have an opinion or make any decisions. That's how I saw it through my teenage years. Of course I get it now. It wasn't anything to do with me. It was to do with them. They were two people who had met, fallen in love, had a kid, and now had fallen out of love again.

I don't know if anyone else was involved. I never asked and was never told. I guess Dad might have had a bit on the side, but, like I say, I don't know.

I was just told that we were moving – going to a flat in a town twenty miles away from home. I was excited – and nervous – but mostly excited. It was an adventure: moving from this little town to somewhere bigger; from a house to a flat; from all that I knew to the complete unknown.

On the day of the move things were still normal. Dad went off to work, leaving Mum and me in a house full of boxes. I went off to school while she waited in for the moving men, and then at the end of the day she came and got me from school and we drove away from here to our new place.

Some of our stuff was there, but not all of it. And Dad didn't come home that night.

I asked Mum about it and she sat me down and told me the usual spiel: that 'Mummy and Daddy didn't love each other anymore' but that they still loved me 'very, very much' and I would 'still see

Daddy a lot, maybe even more than before' because I could go and stay with him and we could have 'boys' weekends', and that it would just be Mummy and me living in the flat, but we were 'going to have such fun!'

Well, I remember the conversation, but I don't really remember my reaction. From all reports I didn't take it well, to say the least. I was a tantrum machine for days, my mum told me later. But, like I say, I can't really remember.

I do remember that I hated that flat. It probably wasn't so bad. My bedroom was even bigger than the one you have here. And if you have to share it with your sister it's probably pretty cramped. But it wasn't about space, it was about what the place represented to me.

I think, in my mind, I'd got things the wrong way round. I figured that we had moved to this flat, but there wasn't room enough for Dad, and that's why he wasn't living with us anymore. And because he couldn't live with us anymore, he'd stopped loving my mum.

So it was the flat's fault.

Oh, I should say, that I never had a single 'boys' weekend' with my dad. I saw him for a few days and nights in the first year, then he got a job in Australia – I think maybe he was trying to get as far away as possible. I haven't seen him since, and you know what? I don't care. I really don't.

I was arrested for the first time when I was twelve. Well, not arrested, but taken to the police station to be given a stern talking to about kicking over people's bins and posting their rubbish back to them through their letter boxes.

The next time – and that was a proper arrest – was for drinking and fighting. I was fourteen. I paid a fine.

When I was sixteen I spent two months in a youth prison for being found in possession of a knife. I was just about to stick it into someone when the police caught me. Good job they did, or I might have gone through with it and ended up with a much longer sentence.

The fine didn't do anything to stop me, but being in prison? Yeah, that did it.

Despite my time in there, I still managed to get my GCSEs. It was good timing. I'd done most of the work, but the exams were still far enough off. You can get a hell of a lot of revision done in a prison library, you know?

So I got into sixth form and, I don't know whether it was the shock of prison, the fact that I was doing something more interesting than standard school lessons, or a drop in hormones, but I straightened out.

I was really not a very nice person as a teenager. I broke my mum's heart – she told me – but I barely saw her. From the moment we moved into that flat – the flat that killed my parents' marriage, as I saw it – I spent as little time there as I could.

That knife – the one that got me sent away – I pulled it on my mum one night when she tried to stop me from going out. Don't know where I was going, or why it was so important. Probably drinking. Maybe fighting. Almost certainly hanging around on a street corner somewhere. Dead important. Important enough to threaten to stab your own mother.

God, I was a shit.

But, like I say, sixth form sorted me out. Maybe it was because I got to study the things that really interested me – history, economics, politics – and maybe it was that I didn't have to be there every hour of every day, being patronised by teachers. Hey, I even had a couple of days where I didn't have to be in until nearly lunchtime. That was very cool.

Maybe it was the shock of prison, making me want to stay out of there – which I have, since then.

And maybe it was Colleen.

13.

She was a vision in black when she walked into that first politics class. I had heard of these things called 'Emos' and wondered if that was what she was going for, but before I got a chance to speak to her, a lad asked her if she was one and she slapped him full across the face. "I'm a fucking Goth, you moron!" she said, as he cradled his reddening cheek.

I tell you, it was love at first sight.

She used to hate it when I told that story. She said it made her sound like a brainless thug, when it was actually someone from her old school that she had a score to settle with. I prefer to tell it without context. I think it makes her sound awesome.

She wasn't a brainless thug, of course. How could I fall for someone like that? No, she was beautiful, insightful, kind, patient, passionate, and had a short fuse for people who pushed her too far.

She sat next to me on that first day, and while I

was just trying to understand the concepts the tutor was outlining, she was already asking questions and pushing what she called her 'radical anarcho-socialist agenda'. It basically meant that she wanted to get rid of the government and have a system where everybody worked for themselves and for each other, for the betterment of mankind.

Or something.

To be honest, I never really understood, and I don't think she did, entirely. The tutor fell in love with her too, though. He had someone to argue with, and she was never shy about doing that.

I still don't know why she chose to sit next to me that first day. There were plenty of other empty seats in the room but she took the one next to me, introduced herself, and started talking to me like we were old friends.

I think I'd already fallen for her by the end of that first lesson.

We went out together that night, with a bunch of others – mostly her friends and one or two others who we'd met that day. There was a whole group of us, but we always counted it as our first date. Why not? It was the first time we kissed after all, however sloppily and however drunkenly.

After that, we always sat together in our classes – politics and history. She took English where I took economics. She always said that she couldn't be bothered with all those numbers, but I've seen her work out the individual totals for a table of twelve before the waiter even brought the bill. She could do the maths okay, she just loved books and words more, and that was fine with me.

When we didn't have classes, we would sit together and study, or talk, or listen to music – she had a splitter thing for the headphones for her CD player. Or we'd find a secluded place to snog, or we'd just go for walks.

Those two years of college were pretty near idyllic. At least, they were when I was at college with her.

At the end of every day, though, when we finally had to go home – because we'd run out of money and it was just too cold to hang around – we each left with heavy feet. It wasn't just that we wanted to be together. It was that we didn't want to go back to what was waiting for us.

I'd straightened out, it's true, and was no longer getting into trouble, but that didn't mean that I'd fallen in love with the flat – that I'd forgiven it. And I hadn't forgiven my mum either. I didn't pull a knife on her again, but I wasn't kind to her, wasn't nice or pleasant.

And she had her own problems. She'd managed to find work when we moved to the flat – a job in an office, which paid enough for us to live okay – but we were never rich, and she worked long days.

And of course she had the little ray of joy that was her son to come home to. I'm not surprised she started drinking.

I didn't notice until it had really become a problem. I was too busy lost in my own shit, and being out of the flat as often and for as long as I could.

By the time I came back to myself, became aware of what was happening, she was getting through two bottles of wine every evening. I tried to talk to her about it, but I didn't know what to say.

It didn't help, anyway. By the time I finished at college, I was starting to find bottles everywhere around the house. And not wine, but vodka and gin. I have no idea how much she was getting through, but during my first year at university I got called home because she'd been taken into hospital.

I blamed the flat.

14.

I didn't know what was happening with Colleen during those years, I just knew that she never wanted to go home either. I probably believed she just didn't want to leave me. I found out what was happening the first time we had a friend's flat to ourselves and could finally do something more than a bit of heavy petting in the park.

Now, don't pull that face, I'm not going to tell you any graphic details. But when we started to take our clothes off, she made me turn out the lights. I did, but there was still enough light coming in from the street for me to see the bruises.

They were all down her arms, a couple on her thighs, and some on her stomach. I realised in that moment why she had always worn long sleeves and skirts. I also realised that I had enough rage inside me to want to kill someone.

She had prepared herself. She knew I was going to ask. She told me.

It was her dad. Like my mum he had his own

problems with alcohol. But where my mum cried and slept, her dad got angry and lashed out.

Colleen grew up listening to him taking it out on her mum. When she got old enough, she put herself in the firing line to save her mum.

She cried when she told me about it, and I held her, running my fingers over her damaged skin. Later, we made love, and it was so gentle.

I was only ever gentle with her. I wanted to be the man who would never hurt her.

When her dad died in our last term, I wondered if she had finally snapped and killed him. But it turns out he fell into the road, drunk, and was run over.

It couldn't have happened to a nicer man.

15.

So we did our A-levels, and both got our grades. We talked about going to the same university, so we could be together, but took what we thought was a rational adult decision to go to the best places, rather than compromise. So, we had that last summer together, and then we officially split up.

We'd agreed that, after our three years, if we hadn't found anyone else, and we still wanted to, we'd see about getting back together.

It sounds so stupid to me when I say it now, and even at the time it felt like throwing a coin into a well and following it with a hopeless wish. It's the kind of thing that happens in films, not life.

So I went off to Manchester, and she went to Warwick.

Of course, I came home in the first term when my mum was hospitalised. I didn't go back afterwards. She needed help, and we needed money, so I had to go out and get a job.

Economics turned out to have been an okay choice – politics and history not so much – and I ended up working in a bank.

The work was fine, but dull. I made some friends to drink with. Met a few girls to do a little more, but all the time I was waiting for the holidays. First Christmas came and went, then Easter, and then summer. Colleen didn't come home. Her dad was gone, true, but I think she'd taken the chance to get away and she wasn't going to give it up.

After a year my mum was doing better. Still drinking, but keeping it under control. She went back to work, and I guess I could have re-enrolled, done the university thing at last. But there didn't seem any point. I'd had a promotion at work and was doing okay.

In what would have been my second year, I was doing well enough to get my own flat. It wasn't far from Mum's, so I could come round and check on her. But she'd met a new man, and she didn't seem to need the drink so much, so even that burden was lifted.

Life wasn't exactly good, but it was okay.

The third year passed in a series of days that looked pretty much alike. And then, in the June, nearly three years after I'd said goodbye to her, Colleen was on my doorstep.

She didn't call ahead, and I had no idea that she

knew where I'd moved to, but there she was.

It was a Tuesday evening. I don't know why I remember that. It just seemed incongruous. Our meeting should have been on a Friday, or a Sunday afternoon. Tuesday evening seemed too… normal.

But there she was. I'd just finished eating. The doorbell rang. I opened the door, and there she was.

She had changed. Her hair was no longer black and she was wearing a pale blue sleeveless dress. I had never seen her arms and legs in the light before. It brought a lump to my throat.

She'd cut her hair short. It was red, kinda like yours, but dyed. And she had almost no makeup on.

I know I was gaping. She told me later that it took all her strength not to laugh at me.

I was wearing my work-shirt and trousers, my tie loose round my neck. My shoes were off and I was standing in my socks. And this… vision, was standing at my door, smiling at me.

"Well?" she said, and that was all she had to say. Everything was in that question. Had I found someone else? Did I still want her? Was our deal still on?

I didn't say anything, just stepped out, put my arms around her and kissed her.

16.

We got married the following summer. I was twenty two. That was ten years ago.

I carried on working at the bank. She got a job as an English teacher. We were happy.

We moved out of my flat into a place much like this. I think we planned to do the same thing my parents did, have a couple of years to ourselves and then start a family.

But when we tried, nothing happened.

At first we thought it was bad luck, and we kept trying. That was fun, for a while. But then it became desperate.

So we did the tests and it was me. It wasn't that *we* were unable to have kids. It's that *I* was. She told me it didn't matter, and we talked about adopting, but in the end the subject just went away and we carried on living our lives.

I started drinking. Like mother, like son. It wasn't bad, but it was regular, and it was more than it ought to have been – especially given the lessons of our parents.

Colleen was patient with me, but I could tell she was scared of what might happen.

I wasn't a nasty drunk, though, which I think helped. But I could see in her eyes that she was waiting, always waiting, for the moment when I turned, when I would grip her arms too tightly, when my fist might swing.

It never did. I never hit her. Not once. Not even when she told me she was pregnant and that it wasn't mine.

We argued, we cried, we made up.

She told me it was a fling, a one night thing, and I believed her. I told her I was just happy to have a child, even if it wasn't mine.

I meant it!

But I started drinking more.

I still didn't get violent, or even angry. I never hit her.

But I killed her as surely as if I had.

She was six months pregnant when she went out to buy bleach and cloths to clean up my vomit, and milk to quieten my stomach. It wasn't the first time we'd run out of things in the middle of one of my bouts and she'd had to dash to the shops, but it was the last.

The other driver was drunk – ironic, right? He went straight through a red light and into the driver's side of her car. The police told me she would have been dead instantly, and so would the baby.

When my wife was killed, she was trying to clean up the mess that was her husband. And me? I was lying on the bathroom floor, snoring into my own puke.

17.

That was two years ago.

Obviously, I was a wreck. But my mum looked after me, and for the first time since I was ten, I let her.

She'd stopped drinking when she met Matt. He was good for her. But she'd been there, so she knew what I needed. She knew how to wean me off the drink. How to cope with my reactions to being sober. How to hold me when I cried.

It doesn't matter how old we get, a boy always needs his mother.

And then, six months after Colleen died, on the day I went back to work, Mum was cleaning my house, and she found one of my old stashes. She drank, as far as anyone can tell, a whole bottle of vodka in a single sitting. Her insides ruptured properly, for once and all. I found her dead on my couch when I got home.

Six months after that, the bank decided that I no longer 'fit their profile, going forward', that they were 'restructuring for better customer quality' and that, basically, I was fired.

I had enough money to last me for nearly a year, but last week the bank I used to work for repossessed my house.

And that's it. That's my story. That's how I end up at thirty two with no job, no house, no father, a wife, a baby and a mother who I loved, and who I as much as killed, and no hope. I only had enough money left to buy the train ticket to get here and this gun – which was easier than it ought to be: they should do something about that.

So, I've got nothing, literally nothing except what I'm wearing, and nothing to live for.

So, go on, tell me what else I should have planned to do?

18.

Keira sat and listened while Toby talked. She didn't interrupt, and she barely shifted in her seat. All that happened was that, as he told his story, her gaze dropped from his face, to his feet, to the floor, and finally to the hands curled in her lap. When he finished, she didn't answer his question, and still didn't move or raise her head. She sat in silence while one minute became two, and then she rose to her feet and walked out of the room.

Toby watched her leave, and listened to her feet as they crossed the landing to her bedroom. He waited, wondering if she was going to come back.

He'd never told the whole of his story before. Not like that. Most people he might have spoken to would know part of it, they would know about one death or the other. They would know about his life with Colleen or his troubled teenage years. He had never had to go right back and tell it all in this way.

He guessed he should feel cleansed, as though a weight had been lifted. If the shrinks were right about the 'talking cure' then surely he should now be bouncing around, full of the joys of the world, casting his gun away and declaring his intention to live forever.

Instead he could still feel the burden of everything bearing down on him, but now he could feel the exact shape of it: the corners and edges pressing in on him, confining him, forcing him in his singular direction.

When Keira didn't return after five minutes – in fact, there was no sound from her room at all – he thought about going after her, but it just felt too hard to stand and follow.

After another long five minutes, Toby felt his earlier panic start to return. He was aware that time was moving on and, if he wasn't going to go through with the job which had brought him here, he probably needed to leave before Keira's mother came home. The girl had seemingly accepted his presence as normal, but he doubted her mother would feel the same way. He needed to know if she would let him leave now. While he had nowhere else to go, he really didn't want to be sent to prison again, and certainly not for something which he hadn't even done.

He pushed himself to his feet, feeling aged and heavy, and walked from the bedroom.

When he first entered the house, he hadn't spent much time looking at the landing, but now, the sense of déjà vu as he saw the familiar hallway, was almost overwhelming. The light came in from the long window on the left and shone off the faux-wooden panels on the bathroom door. That, at least, hadn't changed, though he noticed with gratitude that the horrendous carpet he remembered from his childhood had been replaced.

At the other end of the hallway, the door to what had been his bedroom was ajar, and inside he could see the edge of a wardrobe and a t-shirt on the floor.

He paced along the landing, and placed his hand on the door, allowing it to swing open under his touch.

He stepped inside. It was still the room he remembered, but there was no wave of recollection to fall on him this time. It was too different. It was the same space, with the same view, but the contents of the room were completely different. This was someone else's room now.

Keira had shed her jacket and torn t-shirt and put on a dressing gown in a thick, fleecy, dark purple. Then she had curled up on the bed which occupied the furthest corner. Her back was to Toby, and she was making almost no noise, but he could tell from the shaking of her shoulders that she was crying.

He felt awkward, unsure what to do, and then instinct moved him forward and he walked across the room and sat down on the edge of the bed.

She didn't react though she must have felt the mattress shift under her.

Toby reached out his hand and placed it on her shoulder. She stiffened for a moment, and her breath caught in gasp, but then she relaxed and he felt her silent sobbing subside into breathing.

Toby sat there, with his hand on her, while she calmed, and at one point he wondered if she had gone to sleep. But then she spoke.

"Your story was sad," she said.

Toby's hand squeezed her shoulder a little, in reassurance. Her voice had lost all of the bluster and assurance of earlier, and she sounded like what she was: a child.

"I know," he said, "I'm sorry." He felt a wave of guilt at having burdened her with his woes. Her confident front had made it easy for him to forget how young she really was, and as he thought about all he had told her he realised that there was no way his tale had been appropriate for a girl her age.

"S'okay," she said. "I asked for it."

He nodded, then realised she couldn't see him and said, "I know. But I'm sorry anyway."

"S'okay," she said again, and then was silent.

They sat like that for a while, then she shifted slightly, turning her head so she could look up at him. "But it wasn't just your story. It's other stuff."

That wasn't a surprise to Toby. He knew there

was something going on with this girl, and he guessed hearing his troubles had reminded her of whatever that was.

She gave a small smile, and Toby saw a flicker of her earlier confidence in it, a confidence which he now wondered about. Was it really just a wall to keep the world out?

"There's something wrong with this room," she said. "If you can work it out, I'll tell you."

19.

Toby looked at her for a moment longer, and her smile widened and she nodded. She seemed okay. Perhaps he hadn't caused any lasting damage.

He shifted his gaze to the room.

It was a teenage bedroom. There were clothes on the floor mixed in with cases for DVDs and Xbox games, empty glasses with traces of their previous contents, and various school books. The far wall was occupied by a wardrobe, which had Keira's jacket hanging from its handle, and a spill of clothes emerging from its open door. The doors themselves were covered with stickers from some cartoon or other; a remnant of an earlier age, Toby presumed. In the corner next to that was a small flatscreen TV, with the Xbox on the floor in front of it, and against the other wall was an old toy box. Under the window was a desk with a laptop computer in the centre, surrounded by books and assorted pens and pencils, empty mugs and sweet wrappers. Then came the bed, nestled in the corner against the fitted wardrobes which he remembered making a good hiding place when he was playing with his friends so many years ago.

There were posters all over the walls, most of them labelled NIN or Nine Inch Nails, but they were fastened to wallpaper which was a lurid pink, with princesses on it. Like the stickers on the wardrobe it was a remnant of a childhood that had not yet been expunged.

Nothing seemed out of place. Nothing seemed 'wrong'. He looked back down at Keira. Her eyes were wider, and some colour had returned to her cheeks. She was watching him expectantly. She nodded toward the rest of the room. "Go on," she said.

Toby stood up and wandered around the available floorspace, careful not step on any of the detritus. It looked like a perfectly normal teenaged girl's room, as far as he could tell.

He stepped up to the desk and peered out of the window. The view was just as he remembered it, though the trees were taller and the neighbours on the left had installed decking.

As he stepped back, he saw something out of the corner of his eye, and paused. He peered down behind the desk. It was butted up against the radiator, and behind that he saw something he recognised.

"Is this it?" he asked, pointing.

"Is what it?" Keira asked. She had rolled over on the bed to follow his progress.

He pointed again, and looked down at the rectangle of Postman Pat wallpaper that had been left behind the radiator when the room had been redecorated. That had been his wallpaper when this had been his room. He had forgotten all about it until now.

Keira laughed, and Toby was glad to hear it. "Oh, yeah, that must have been yours, yeah? Postman Pat, eh? Rock and roll!" She swung her legs off the bed and sat up. "Nope that's not it. Don't think about what is here. Think about what isn't."

As she prompted him, the laughter dropped out of her voice.

He turned and faced into the room. He tried to think what should be here, and wasn't. It seemed that she had everything she could need for a comfortable life.

And then he realised, and felt a cold spike in his stomach. She'd been dropping clues, whether she knew that or not, and they'd been niggling at him, but only now did he realise what they were.

He looked across at Keira and from the look on her face, she knew he had worked it out.

He needed to say it, though. She needed to tell him, it was clear, but she also needed to feel that she was being forced.

"You said your favourite number was seventeen?" he asked.

She nodded, he face sombre, her lips pressed tightly together.

"Your sister. You said you had a sister who was seventeen. There's no second bed though. This is your room, not a shared one. Where is she? What happened to her?"

20.

Yeah, so she's dead.

I told you that she was seventeen when we were just talking. But that's how old she would have been. She was four when I was born and I was four when she died. She was in the car with Dad.

People tell you that you can't really remember things from when you're little. You know, when you're three or two, or whatever. But they're wrong.

On the other hand some people claim to remember being born, and I think they're full of shit. But I remember my sister. Not just from photos and things, but from real life. Memories that don't have photos, you know?

They might just be from when I was four, in the months before she died, but I think I remember more, going back a couple of years.

She was taller than me. I know that was cos she was older, but it always seems important. When I think what she would look like now, I think she would be tall.

She'd be seventeen so she'd be, like, almost all the way grown up, and I think she'd be tall and elegant. I'm short and stumpy, and she'd be all the way up there.

I guess she wouldn't want to spend time with me if she was still alive. And she'd hate having to share this room with me. Can you imagine? Can you imagine how crushed we'd be in here? I bet we'd fight all the time and she'd be bored and annoyed by her little sister always hanging around.

But, you know, that'd be okay. Better than the alternative.

She had blonde hair. I did too, when I was little, before it turned ginger. But I think she would have stayed blonde. And she wouldn't have cut it like I do, she'd have let it grow and it would be down to the middle of her back.

She'd be so beautiful now. So it's probably good that she's not here, cos I'd just be dead jealous all the time. And she'd have fit boyfriends, who would think I was funny while I tried to get their attention, and then think I was annoying when they wanted to get Christine alone.

She'd be dead clever too. Much cleverer than those dull boyfriends she keeps bringing around. They look nice, but they're always just a bit thick.

Why is it that good looking guys are always stupid? Is it because when they're good looking they don't have to try hard to get what they want, so they don't bother, and their brains don't develop?

Of course some boys are good looking and don't know that they're good looking. They might develop their brains and then end up with both. That'd be okay, I guess.

I think that's what Christine is like. I think she's always been beautiful but maybe, when she was about ten, she needed braces or something. I had them, they were a real pain – always got food stuck in them, or the wires would dig into your cheeks or something. I had mine off last year. So, yeah, I think she had those, and they made her all self-conscious, and she thought she was ugly. So she got her head down, and worked hard, trying to make up for a problem that wasn't there. And now she's starting to realise that she's grown up and beautiful, but she's also got the brains to really do something.

Maybe she has dumb boyfriends because she likes to be able to control them. But that sounds a bit manipulative. I think it's a self-consciousness thing. I think she's not yet confident to pick the guy she wants, so she settles for the ones who pick her. And I think she's so beautiful that only the good looking guys – who are, as I said, real dumbos – are willing to try. When she gets to university she'll meet different guys, and she'll find someone there who will be good looking – but not too good looking – and also smart. He'll probably be called Ethan or Joel or, who knows, maybe Toby. And he'll make a good big brother-in-law for me, and always have my back.

She's good at whatever she wants to be good at, so I think she's studying Maths and English and Art at A-level. That way she can do whatever she wants. She'll probably do one of those joint degrees in something like English and Economics – like you did – and then she'll be a teacher maybe, or work somewhere important. She'll move to London with Ethan and they'll have a really cool flat where I can go and visit and go to the shows and go shopping with her and then go for pizza and late night drinks in some posh wine bar.

It's all going to work out for her.

Or, well. Yeah, okay, you can stop looking at me like that. I know what I'm saying. I'm not loopy. I know she's dead and none of this ever happened and none of it ever will. But I like to think about all these things, okay? I like to think about the life she never go to live because of that fucking idiot, okay? Is that a crime? If it is, lock me up.

21.

Like I say, I was four when she died, but I do still remember her, I really do. She was eight years old and she was my big sister, and I loved her and she loved me.

We shared this room. My bed was here, where it is now, where it's always been. Her bed was over there, where the TV is. The wardrobe wasn't there then.

We used to play in here, or in the garden. It was her that dug up your crown. She found it, and then she gave it to me. I remember her doing it. We had a ceremony and she crowned me and told me I was a princess. I used to like princesses if you hadn't already guessed.

I can't have been more than three, but I remember it. I remember my mum shouting at the both of us for getting so muddy from the digging and from playing with a crown covered in dirt. I remember it. I remember her.

I wonder, sometimes, if I can remember that far back because she died. People say that, don't they, that you forget things because you write new memories over the old ones. But if you want to remember something, you have keep going back to the memories, cos then you rewrite them. You remember remembering them, so they become new memories again.

And I keep remembering Christine. I keep remembering her. I remember my birthdays – at least two of them. One of them we went to a funfair, and she rode with me on the big wheel, holding my hand cos I was a bit scared. Another one we had a party here in the house, and it was raining like crazy outside, even though it was summer – my birthday's in June. We didn't care, we went outside and ran around anyway, me and her and my friends, and I thought that Mum would shout at us for getting so wet, but because it was my birthday she just laughed and said it was okay.

That was my fourth birthday, I think; the last one before Christine died; the last one before he killed her.

Because that's what happened, and it's why I don't like to think about my dad and why I don't really remember him.

I remember Christine, but I don't remember him.

He was driving. The car crashed. They both died. He was drunk.

That was why I was upset. I mean, your story was sad and all that. Hell, it was horrible. I'm not surprised you want to kill yourself. I'm amazed you've lasted this long.

But when you talked about your wife, and your baby, it was just like my dad, but it was the other way around. He'd had a load to drink and then gone to pick up Christine from her ballet class.

She was a wonderful dancer, and she would have been even better if, you know, it hadn't happened.

Of course, now I'm grown up I'd laugh at the idea of being a ballet dancer. But when she was dressed up in her leotard and her shoes, with her blonde hair tied up the way they do, I remember I just wanted to be her.

I was too young, though. Mum said that when I was older, if I still wanted, I could take lessons too. But by then Christine was gone, and I didn't want to do it, because she couldn't do it anymore. And it wouldn't be any fun on my own.

So I never became a dancer. Never really became anything.

I remember the funeral. It was awful. There were two boxes together at the front, and I remember screaming for her to come home.

She didn't though. She couldn't. And she never will.

22.

So that was that. That was me, four years old, not even started school yet and Daddy was dead and he'd taken Christine with him. You wonder why I never want to think of him? You want to know why I could never forgive him?

Course you don't. You understand. When you were telling your story, I could feel where it was going. Stories like that – especially when they lead to you sitting in a stranger's bedroom with a gun in your mouth – only end one way. I could feel your story in my guts, curling round, getting ready to pounce or scream or something. If you had told me that it was your fault, that you'd been driving and you'd killed your wife and your baby, then I don't know what I would have done. I might have tried to get that gun off you and kill you myself. It would have been revenge, I guess.

But you didn't. Not like my daddy did. You were just, I dunno, weak. You were lying on the floor and it was some other arsehole. Someone like Daddy, who did it. You weren't to blame. But he was. He was driving, and he was drunk – with an eight year old in the car! – and he ran into a tree.

I've asked Mum since, and she said that the police had told her there was no-one else involved. There was no car coming the wrong way down the street, causing him to swerve. No little boys running out after a ball. No dogs or cats dashing home that he gave his life for. Nope. Just a drunk dickhead who couldn't drive down a straight road without hitting a tree.

Do you know what it's like to go to your sister's funeral when you're only four years old? And you wonder why I wanted a share of your gun.

When I saw you had that thing I thought it was kinda cool. I know, I'm a stupid kid. But when I worked out why you had it, I wanted what you wanted.

You see, I worked it out while you were telling your story. Oh, I probably worked it out years ago. I've probably known it for ages. But you see, life is pointless. It's rubbish. There is no reason for any of us to be alive. So, why go on?

23.

On my ninth birthday, I wouldn't let Mummy throw me a party. She wanted to, just as she had ever since Christine and Daddy died. But I didn't want it. And I haven't wanted one since. Why should I? She was eight when she died. Should I celebrate because I managed to beat her? Because I managed to make it through more life than she did before she was murdered by her own Dad? No, don't be fucking stupid. Of course not.

So I've been counting time. I've been counting the years and the months and the days. I have now lived through one thousand seven hundred and ninety one days that my sister never had.

I got to turn nine, and ten, and eleven. I got to leave our crappy junior school – the one up the road, the one you probably went to – and I got to move up to the big school – just as crap, only bigger. I got to turn twelve, and then thirteen. I got to be a teenager.

I got to live in a world where everyone has a mobile phone, but if the one you get is too nice, someone will be happy to stab you to take it away. I got to live in a world of internet stalking and sexting. I got to be old enough to have a Facebook account of my very own. Christine didn't even live long enough to know what Facebook was, or why it's such a waste of fucking time.

I get to live in a world of global warming, and global terror, and global financial meltdowns, and all I can think is that she was the lucky one. She escaped when she was still young enough not to care. She escaped before it all went horribly wrong. She escaped and she left me behind.

And so I don't care.

I listen to my music loud, because it drowns out the world. I cut my hair short because it will never be long and blonde. And I do this too.

They fade over time, but I make sure there are always eight cuts showing. Mum doesn't know. I always wear long sleeves, or my jacket – she complains about that – and she doesn't see me when I shower. She thinks I'm being private, but I just don't want her to see the cuts.

I've read about self-harming, and why people do it, and I don't think it's the same. I don't do it to feel alive, like I've read about, where the pain makes the world feel real. I do it to remember. One cut for each year she was alive. And each time I do it I try to pull up a new memory, one that's just on the edge of disappearing, so that I can hold onto it; hold onto her.

I don't want to slash my wrists or anything. That would be too messy. I don't cut deep, that's why they fade. But I make sure I do it. I check them every day and if one needs doing, it gets done. Can't even remember how long I've been at it. Guess I've written over the memory of the first time with all the times after. But I can remember Christine.

And it's everything to me now. Do you get it? My life isn't my life, it's a memorial to my sister. That's all that life is to me. It's me keeping her memory alive.

It's the same for my mum. She died on that day too.

Well, not really. I mean, she's still alive and that, but part of her died. She's never been happy since, not really. She's never thrown herself into the day the way she used to. She notices me, but not like she used to. Even when she tells me off, she doesn't really seem to care.

And if she doesn't, then why should I?

She should be with us here, now. We could take your gun and go back into her room and we could all be finished with it.

Come on. Let's go and wait for her. Come on.

24.

Keira grabbed at Toby's hands, her sleeves falling back down to hide the thin red lines, four on the inside of each arm, and she tried to tug him to his feet.

She had stood up while she talked, and Toby had taken her place, sitting on the edge of the bed, while she paced.

He had wanted to interrupt at several points, but he remembered that she had listened to him tell his tale, all the way through, and he gave her the same courtesy. But he could see her working herself up into a frenzy, and it worried him.

When she came over and tried to pull him up, tried to get him to accompany her to her mother's bedroom to engage in a suicide pact, he braced his feet on the floor, and refused to be budged.

She pulled and pulled, her own feet slipping the carpet, pulling her closer to him. He said nothing. He just let her pull and waited for what he knew was coming.

It took longer than he expected, and his hands

and feet were starting to get tired. But her excited requests turned to shouting, and then finally the dam broke.

She started to cry, loud braying sobs mixed with pleading and cursing. Her tugging grew weaker, and then she collapsed forward and he opened his arms to catch her.

She hooked her chin over his shoulder, screaming out her grief, and wrapped her arms around him as he did the same to her. Her knees buckled and he grabbed her legs and swung them up so she was sitting sideways on his lap, her arms around his neck, and her tears running down his back.

He started to cry too. His was quieter, and the tears squeezed from his eyes like individual drops of pain. If asked he wouldn't have been able to tell if he was crying for himself, and all that he had lost, or if he was crying for her.

Maybe he was crying for everyone. Everyone who had ever loved and lost. Everyone who had ever made a mistake. Everyone who had hit bottom and then tried to dig deeper.

His tears were hot and hard and didn't last long. He'd already cried enough. But hers continued, a storm which had been a long time coming and had built up a lot of pressure. He held her until her sobs started to break down into whimpers, and then continued to hold her until even they petered out.

Finally they were just sitting on the bed, her with her arms around him, both breathing deeply.

She stirred and pulled her head back. Her eyes were red and her face blotchy. Tears and snot streaked her skin, but she managed a small smile.

"Not how you expected your day to go?" she asked, and he smiled back and shook his head.

"You can let me go now," she added, swinging her legs round and pulling free from his embrace. She looked embarrassed.

She straightened her dressing gown, wiped her nose and mouth on the sleeve, and then scrubbed her hands over her face. She looked up at him. "No final solution, then? No grand gesture?"

"No," Toby said. "I don't think so. Not today."

She nodded. "Guess not." She looked around the room. "So, what now?"

25.

Toby stood up and took another look around the room, remembering when it was his. Then he turned his gaze to one item in particular. "What else have you got in your toy-box?" he asked.

Keira looked at the box then back at Toby. "Why?"

"You said you kept the crown in your treasure chest. I reckon that box is it. You keep your treasure in it – your sister's things, I'm guessing – so I just wondered what else you have."

Keira shrugged. "Not too bad at the old Sherlock thing yourself, are you?" she said as she went over and knelt in front of the box. Toby pulled the chair away from the desk and sat down behind her.

It wasn't a real chest, but just an old box painted white, with handles on the side, and an ill-fitting lid. She lifted this off and delved inside.

The first things she brought out were exactly what Toby had been expecting: a pair of ballet shoes. She passed them to him and he took them with care.

"These were hers," he said, and she nodded, watching him holding them and biting her bottom lip.

"Did you ever try them on?" he asked.

Keira shook her head.

"Not good enough to fill her shoes?"

Keira shrugged.

He placed the shoes on the desk. "What else?"

Keira handed him a ball made from interlocking hair scrunchies and ties. He didn't say anything. It was obvious what they were. He looked at them and then put them with the shoes.

The next thing she handed up to him was a small, yellow teddy bear. It was cheaply made and had been loved hard. The fur was bald in places, and some of the stitching had given way.

"Hers again?" Toby asked.

"She won it at the fair, on my birthday. She got a ping-pong ball into a jar. She was always good at shit like that. She took it to bed with her every night. When she… was gone, it was the only one of her toys I wanted to keep. The rest came from other people, but that one she got because of me. And she loved it most. So I wanted that one."

Each of the items was no more or less than what he had expected, but they made Toby sad. This was meant to be a toy-box, the word was even written in faded red paint on the lid. It was meant to hold a child's favourite things, but this one had become a mausoleum, a reliquary.

He sat the teddy up with its back leaning against the ballet shoes and he leant forward to look over Keira's shoulder into the box.

"What's that?" he asked, pointing to a smaller box in the corner.

"That? Oh, that's nothing."

"Go on. Show me. What is it?"

Keira reached in and took the box out. It was about a foot square and maybe six inches deep, made out of a rich dark wood, nicely finished.

"What's in it?" Toby asked, and Keira opened it.

The inside of the box was lined with crushed velvet and, nestled inside were the pieces of a clarinet.

"Whose is that?" he asked.

Keira didn't say anything for a few moments and then murmured, "Mine."

"Can I see?" Toby asked, holding out his hands. She passed him the box and he looked more closely at the parts of the instrument. Tucked inside the lid were sheets of paper.

He pulled them out and unfolded them.

"Aw, no. Don't," said Keira, but she made no move to stop him.

They were certificates, printed on thick, expensive paper. They informed anyone reading them that Keira Nolan had achieved grades one through five in the clarinet, with merits in all of them except grade four in which she had got a distinction. The last one was just over a year old.

"Wow, you must be pretty good," Toby said.

Keira just shrugged. "Not bad."

"You still play."

"Not for a while. And don't ask me to, cos I won't."

"No, that's okay. You grew out of it, and it got dull, I guess?" He gave the girl a smile, and she half-returned it.

"Yeah, pretty much. It was something they had me do at school – my old school. I kept going long enough to get grade five, but my new school didn't care, so I didn't see why I should."

"But you kept it."

"What?"

Toby pointed to the toy-box. "You kept your clarinet and your certificates. And you didn't just keep them, you kept them in your treasure chest. So they mean something to you. Something more than just a thing you used to do that you don't care about any more."

Another shrug. "I guess."

"You kept them in the box with all the things you care about. All of Christine's things."

Keira's brow furrowed. "Yeah, so?"

Toby placed a hand on her shoulder. She was getting defensive and he didn't want it to turn into anger. "So you did something in your life that you thought was important. Something that you thought was at least important enough to rank with the things that your sister did, that your sister was. You said before that your whole life was just a memory of hers. But this is something that was entirely you. Something you were good at. Something you were proud of. Something you thought was worth keeping hold of. Did your sister play an instrument?"

Keira shook off his hand and pulled away. "Of course she didn't. She never had time. She was dead before she got the chance."

Toby held up his hands. "Okay, okay. Yes, she never got the chance. But you did. You got the chance to do something, to have a life of your own that wasn't entirely about her. And, at least for a while, you took that chance."

Keira stood up and stepped up against the wall. "So, what are you saying? That I was bad, that I didn't remember her? Cos that's not true. I've never forgotten her. Never!"

Toby pushed back, the wheels of the chair dragging on the carpet as he gave her some room. "That's not what I'm saying. I'm saying that it's okay. You have a life, and you're allowed to live it. Christine wouldn't want you to be sad, or to live every day in memory of her."

"How do you know? You never met her!"

"Trust me, I know. From what you told me, she loved her life, yes?"

Keira nodded, her lips thin and tight, her head down, her eyes boring into his.

"Of course she did. She loved her ballet and going to fairs with her sister, and digging in the dirt for treasure and getting covered in mud."

Keira's eyes filmed with tears as Toby prodded her memories again. "But from everything you told me, there's one other thing she loved."

"What?"

"You. She loved you. Every memory you told me about tells me that she loved you very much. And she wouldn't want you to be in pain. She wouldn't want you to cut yourself or kill yourself. She'd want you to live each day in happiness and joy that she was ever alive. She'd want you to go on as long as you could, counting the days if you want to, but treating each one as a gift, not a sentence."

The tears spilled over Keira's bottom eyelids and cut fresh tracks down her cheeks. "But how can I?" she asked.

"By doing what you've been doing. By trying new things, experiencing the world, embracing the possibilities. By playing the clarinet, or not playing it. By listening to Nine Inch Nails or One Direction or whoever you like and stuff anyone who says otherwise. By being you, every day, every minute, to the best of your ability. And by showing life that it can beat you and hurt you but it can never end you."

Keira gazed at him, and her body started to relax a little. Her shoulders dropped and her head came up. "This from the man with the gun in his pocket who was planning on blowing his brains out all over my mum's bed just a little while ago?"

Toby laughed. "Yeah, well, I think we both know that's not going to happen now, don't we?"

"Why not?"

He raised a hand and pointed straight at Keira. "Because of you."

26.

"What? What did I do? I was all in favour of you killing yourself. I even said so. You have a great reason, after all. And if you don't, you've got nothing left, so what would you do anyway?"

Toby's eyes opened wide, surprised at hearing his situation laid out in so bald a fashion. He stood up from the chair and turned to stand behind it.

"Well, yes, that's true. And I'm going to have to do some serious thinking about that. But that's what I'm going to do. I'm not going to try and kill myself. That's done with now. I suppose I can probably get some money for the gun – hell, maybe I can get a refund – and then I'll go on from there."

Keira stepped away from the wall. "But why? What changed your mind? What did I do?"

Toby smiled at her. She tried to play so tough and act so much older than her years, but she was still just a kid. "You didn't have to do anything, other than tell me your story. It was like seeing myself in a mirror. Okay, yes, you're right. I've got every reason in the world to want to end my life, to step off the merry-go-round and just give up. But then again, so have you — at least if you told me the truth."

"I did. I really did. More truth than I've ever told anyone."

"There you go then. So, I should probably have given in to your request. One bullet for you, one for me. And one for your mum if she wanted it."

Keira winced as he reminded her of that part of her plan.

"But, you see," Toby continued, "once it came to it, and I'd heard all of your troubles, I didn't think, 'Great! She's just like me. Now I don't have to die alone: we can do it together!' No, I just thought that I didn't want you to die. I thought that despite all the troubles, you'd managed to live for nine more years with all that pain inside you and that maybe you could live for nine more, or ninety. And that that would be the right thing to do. I didn't want you to die. The idea horrified me. I wanted you to live."

Toby could feel his own tears coming back, so he stopped looking at Keira as he spoke.

He stepped away and looked out of the window at the familiar view.

"And if I didn't want you to die, and thought that it would be better for you to keep on living and try to make your life better, then how could I want anything else for me? By meeting you, I got to see myself from the outside – to see me and my problems as other people would see them – and I realised that I also need to keep on living, and trying to make my life better. I don't know how I'm going to do it, either in terms of money, or somewhere to live, or just keeping myself from crying all the time. But I'm going to find a way. And so are you."

27.

Keira didn't say anything in response, and Toby didn't look to see what her face was saying, he just kept staring out of the back window at the trees that lined the end of the garden. They were tall now, with thick trunks, but he remembered when they were young and the main branches were low enough that he could swing on them, which he loved to do despite his mum shouting at him. When he was a bit older, he was even able to climb up onto them and see into the back garden of the house behind them, and reach up to pinch some of the small, sour apples that grew from their trees.

He wasn't aware that Keira had moved until he felt her small hand slip into his. He looked down and she was standing next to him, looking out of the window too.

"So that's it, then?" she asked, eventually.

"I guess so."

"You'll probably want to go. Mum'll be home in a bit."

"I suppose."

"Are you going to keep in touch?"

"Do you want me to?"

She turned her head and looked up at him. "Yes. I think that's what we need to do. I think you need to keep in touch with me, and I need to keep in touch with you. I think we need to remind each other that we're alive and not let each other take the easy way out. I think that's how this thing works."

Toby nodded. It hadn't been his plan, but it was as good as any.

"Do you believe in God?" Keira asked.

Toby shook his head. "Nope."

Keira nodded. "Nah, me either. So, if I can't count on him, I'll have to count on you."

"And I'll count on you."

"Yep, that's the way it works."

"Okay."

Keira thought for a moment, then said, "Toby?"

"Yeah?"

"I think you'd have been a good dad."

28.

They were half way downstairs, when Toby stopped.

"What, what is it?"

He pointed to the gaps in the banisters, where the staircase was open to the lounge. "Did you ever slip through and jump down from here?"

Keira grinned. "Yeah, course. Did you?"

"All the time. Used to drive my mum batshit."

"Ha! Me too. 'Keira Ashley Nolan, don't you do that! You'll fall and kill yourself!' "

"And did you? Kill yourself?"

"Ha. Nope. You?"

"No, but once, I nearly did. I didn't realise there was a box of Lego underneath me. I fell on that, then fell over, and I broke my arm when I fell."

"Shit!"

"Yep. That's pretty much what I said."

Keira crouched down and looked through the gap in the bannisters. "Did that stop you?"

"Nope."

"Good."

They carried on down the rest of the stairs. But at the bottom, instead of turning towards the front door, Toby turned towards the kitchen.

"What are you doing?"

"Well, if the offer's still there, I could really do with that drink before I go."

Keira followed him in. "You want tea? I make it for mum all the time. She says I make a pretty good cuppa."

Toby shook his head. He was gazing around the room, taking in the fitted cabinets that he remembered so well, and the new cooker which he didn't. "Do you have anything cold? All that talking and crying has really dried out my throat."

"Sure? Is squash okay? It's all we've got."

Toby smiled, thinking of all the cups of squash he had drunk in this very kitchen. "More than okay. It would be perfect."

Keira grabbed a glass from a cupboard and the bottle from the side and made up his drink.

"I can't believe you still have this crappy blue lino," he said as he took a sip.

"I know. Horrible, isn't it?! I keep trying to tell Mum to change it but she won't."

"Well, people fear change. We know that."

"When did you become a wise old hermit?" Keira asked, laughing.

"When I got myself a young apprentice, of course," Toby replied, and sipped more of his drink, trying to look wise and inscrutable. This made Keira laugh even more.

And then a voice came from the hallway. "Keira? Is that you? Have you got a friend here?"

Neither of them had heard the front door, but Keira's mum had arrived home. A moment later, she stepped into the doorway of the kitchen and stopped.

"Who the hell are you?"

Toby rose from his chair. He didn't quite know what to say, but Keira saved him.

"Mum, this is Toby. He used to live here. He asked if he could look around and, as I knew you would be home in a minute, I said okay. It's okay, I haven't let him molest me."

Keira's mum looked at Toby warily and stepped into the room, closer to her daughter. She wasn't much taller than Keira, with shoulder length brown hair. If Toby's quick maths was correct, she must have been early forties at least, but although she looked tired, he didn't think she looked her age. *God, she must have been so young when they bought the house*, Toby thought.

The woman stepped forward and placed herself between her daughter and him. "I'm Barbara, Keira's mother. You really shouldn't have come in, even if she did say it was okay. She's a child. Toby, did you say?"

Toby nodded. "Yes. That's right. I'm sorry. I

didn't think, and she said it was okay."

"She's only thirteen."

"I really am sorry. I'm not a bad man, honestly, and I'm sorry for intruding like this." Barbara was sizing him up, but he could see her starting to relax as he spoke.

"And you used to live here?" she asked.

He nodded again. "That's right. My parents owned this place before you. I was back in town and thought I would see the sights. I was standing outside looking at the old place when your daughter came home from school. She asked me inside. I didn't really want to, not without you present, but she was very insistent. She even forced squash on me."

"Insistent? Well, yes, that sounds like Keira." She looked to her side, where Keira had moved to lean on the sink between them. "And why are you wearing your dressing gown, young lady?"

"My t-shirt got torn. Someone grabbed it on the bus when we went round a corner and they nearly fell over. I didn't think you'd want a stranger ogling my chest, so I put on the thing which would cover as much of me as possible. If that's alright with you."

Barbara didn't respond, just stared at her daughter. Toby could almost hear her counting to ten in her head, and stifled a smile.

Then her gaze was forced back on him. "So,

Toby..." she started, but then her eyebrows narrowed and she peered more closely at him.

After a moment her eyes widened in surprise, her shoulders dropped, and she finally smiled. "I remember you," she said. "You were here when we came to look around the house. You were such a sweet little boy. And you haven't changed much!"

"Mum! Are you flirting with him?" Keira asked, in mock-horror.

Barbara stuttered, flustered. "No. No. Not at all. I just mean. Well, I recognise you because you haven't changed much. And you were a sweet boy when we met. Though I think your parents were trying to hide you because you kept trying to tell us about the leaking tap, and the spiders that lived in the shed, and the crack in the garage floor, and all the things that you're not meant to reveal to potential buyers."

Toby gaped. "I did? I don't remember that!"

"Oh, yes. It was very funny. Ted and I laughed for ages about that. It was one of the reasons we decided to buy it. We figured that any house we bought would have things wrong with it, but at least with you around we had been forewarned, and none of the problems seemed that bad."

"That is amazing!" said Keira.

Barbara looked at Toby and shook her head gently. "How strange to meet you like this."

Toby didn't know what to say, so just smiled and nodded.

Barbara then gave out a gasp and stood up straight, a look of surprise in her eyes.

"What's up, Mum?" Keira asked. Barbara ignored her, her head turning sharply as she looked around the room as though searching for something.

"Ah!" she said at last, and darted towards the sink. She opened the cupboard underneath it and pulled out a large grey tub containing old tins and cans. "It's in here, I think," she said to herself as she rummaged.

Keira stepped across to stand next to Toby, the pair of them watching Barbara in bemusement.

Finally, her search stopped and her hand came out of the depths of the box clutching something. She turned back to face Toby.

"I was digging in the garden the other week. I was planting a rose for...." she trailed off and glanced at her daughter. "For Christine. She was... well... she died. Keira's sister."

Toby didn't know what to say, but knew he shouldn't show that he had already heard the story, so he dipped his eyes and mumbled something that contained the word 'sorry'. Barbara wasn't watching him, but had locked eyes with her daughter. Toby glanced to his side and saw Keira give a nod and a slight smile, and heard Barbara let out a breath.

He looked back at the woman and she was smiling at her daughter. She then turned her smile towards him. "It was her... anniversary." Another look passed between woman and the girl, then Barbara continued. "Anyway, I was digging in the borders at the back, planting a rose, and I found something. It must have been yours. I remember thinking about you. How strange that you should be here now, when I was just thinking about you."

"Mum! You're babbling! Get to the point!" Keira interrupted. She was loud, but she was laughing.

"Yes, sorry. Sorry. So, I put it in the recycling. Didn't really know what to do with it, to be honest. But as you're here, I suppose you should have it back."

She held out her closed fist, and Toby stepped forward, warily holding his hand open under hers. She relaxed her fingers and a small lump of what looked like dirty metal fell into his hand. It was about an inch and a half long, by three-quarters wide. He turned it over, and realised that although the rubber on the wheels had perished, and there was a lot of rust, it was one of his old cars; one of the ones he used to bury in the garden and then dig up again sometime later. This one had been left behind, another small sign that he had left his mark on the world.

Not that long ago – a matter of hours – such a

thing might have made him cry. But, now, it brought a smile to his face instead. He wrapped his own fingers around it, feeling the rough metal digging into his skin, and felt a laugh burst from his mouth.

"Of all the things I thought I'd find here," he said, and then was laughing too much to finish the thought.

Barbara looked a little confused for a moment, but then Keira laughed, and finally Barbara joined them.

It wasn't manic or hysterical, but there was something of a sigh of relief in the shared hilarity.

After a few moments, when they had all calmed down, Barbara looked from Toby to Keira and back again and he could see that she was coming to some sort of decision. "Look, I don't know if you need to get off. But I was about to put some tea on – nothing fancy, just something out of the freezer – but if you want to stay for a bite to eat, I'd love to hear about what you remember of this place. Though madam here might get a bit bored."

"I won't. I promise!" Keira actually jumped as she said it, making both the adults laugh again.

"Okay. So, what do you think?" Barbara asked.

Toby glanced around the room, and thought of all the frozen potato waffles and chicken nuggets he'd eaten here. He reckoned he could manage some more.

"I'd love to," he replied.

Acknowledgements

Thanks are due to those who helped me to write this book. First mention should go to Angi Holden who, back in 2014, asked me to write a novella for a competition (which I didn't win). This was the result.

Thanks, also to Peter Clements, Lorna Connelly, and Dean Rands, my wonderful beta/proof readers.

And, of course, thanks must go to the first reader for all that I do, my wife Kath, for her continued love and support.

Final thanks, to you, Dear Reader. Over the years I have had many people who have read my flash-fictions come back and say, "I loved it, but I wanted more." Well, here's some more. I hope you enjoyed it, and thank you for reading.

Calum Kerr
July 2020

Other books by **Calum Kerr**
from **Gumbo Press**:

Wordsmith

"In the mornings he brings me a word. Gift-wrapped
with love he gives it to me like the reddest rose or the
clearest diamond. This morning he gave me 'murmur'."
- from 'Wordsmith'.

Wordsmith is a short story collection from the master of
flash fiction. Known for his tiny tales of excitement,
adventure, horror and romance, Calum Kerr now
brings us a career-spanning collection of his longer
stories. As you would expect, there is a wide mix of
genres, with stories that will make you smile, cry,
scream and laugh.

31

Containing 31 stories written in the 31 days of January
2011, this collection of flash-fictions spans a wide
range of genres and styles: from science-fiction to an
unconventional love story, from pulp noir to the
apocalypse, from magical realism to the magic of life.

Special Delivery

A new collection of flash fictions from the mind of
Calum Kerr, author of 31, Braking Distance, Lost
Property, the 2014 Collections, and much more. These
stories span Calum's writing career from his very first
flash fiction through to his most recent. And they also
span the full range of stories, from love to death, from
space to suburbia, from the hilarious to the horrific.
Whatever your taste in stories, you'll find something
here to love.

The World in a Flash: How to Write Flash-Fiction

A guide for beginners and experienced writers alike to give you insight into the world of flash-fiction. Chapters focus on a range of aspects, with exercises for you to try.

Undead at Heart

War of the Worlds meets *The Walking Dead* in this novel from Calum Kerr, author of *31* and *Braking Distance*.

The 2014 Flash365 Collections

by Calum Kerr

Apocalypse

It's the end of the world as we know it. Fire is raining from the sky, monsters are rising from the deep, and the human race is caught in the middle.

The Audacious Adventuress

Our intrepid heroine, Lucy Burkhampton, is orphaned and swindled by her evil nemesis, Lord Diehardt. She must seek a way to prove her right to her family's wealth, to defeat her enemy, and more than anything, to stay alive.

The Grandmaster

Unrelated strangers are being murdered in a brutal fashion. Now it's up to crime-scene cleaner Mike Chambers, with the help of the police, to track down the killer and stop the trail of carnage.

Lunch Hour

One office. Many lives. It is that time of day: the time for poorly-filled, pre-packaged sandwiches; the time to run errands you won't have enough time for; the time to fall in love, to kill or be killed, to take advice from an alien. It's the Lunch Hour.

Time

Time. It's running out. It's flying. It's the most precious thing, and yet it never slows, never stops, never waits. In this collection we visit the past, the future, and sometimes a present we no longer recognise. And it's all about time.

In Conversation with Bob and Jim

Bob and Jim have been friends for forty years, but still have plenty to say to each other - usually accompanied by a libation or two. This collection shines a light on an enduring relationship, the ups and downs, and the prospect of oncoming mortality. It is funny and poignant, and entirely told in dialogue.

Saga

One Family. Seven Generations.

Spanning 1865 to 2014, *Saga* follows a single family as it grows and changes. Stories cover war and peace, birth and death, love and loss, are all set against a background of change. More than anything, however, these are stories of people and of family.

Strange is the New Black

Spaceships and aliens, alternative histories and parallel universes, robots, computers, faraway worlds, run-away science and the end of the world; all these and more are the province of science-fiction, and all these and more can be found in this new collection.

The Ultimate Quest

Our heroine Lucy Burkhampton, swindled heiress and traveller through the worlds of literature, is now jumping from genre to genre in search of a mythical figure known only as The Author. Can she reach the real world? Can she escape the deadly clutches of her enemy? Can she finally reclaim her family name?
There's only one way to find out.
Read on...

Christmas

Jeff and Maddie are hosting Christmas this year, for their two boys - Ethan and Jake - for her parents, his father, his brother James and partner Gemma, and for a surprise guest. It's a time of peace and joy, but how long can that last when a family comes together?

Graduation Day

It's Graduation Day, a time for celebration, but for a group of students, their family and their friends, it is going to be a day of terror as the whole ceremony is taken hostage. In the audience sits the target of the terrorists' intentions: Senator Eleanor Thornton. But not far away from her is a man who might just make a difference: former-FBI Agent Jim Sikorski. Can he foil their plans and save the hostages, or will terror rule the day?

Post Apocalypse

Fire fell from the skies, the dead rose from the ground, and aliens watched from orbit as the Great Old Ones enslaved the human race. That was the Apocalypse. This is what happened next. Brandon returns, in thrall, and Todd continues his worship. Jackson finds unconventional ways to fight back, and General Xorle-Jian-Splein takes new control of his mission. The world has ended, but in these 31 flash-fictions, the story continues.

The 2014 Flash365 Anthology
12 Books - 365 New Flash-Fictions
All in one volume.

This book contains:

Apocalypse
The Audacious Adventuress
The Grandmaster
Lunch Hour
Time
In Conversation with Bob and Jim
Saga
Strange is the New Black
The Ultimate Quest
Christmas
Graduation Day
Post Apocalypse

12 books full of tiny stories crossing and mixing genres: crime, science-fiction, horror, stream-of-consciousness, surrealism, comedy, romance, realism, adventure and more. From the end of the world to the start of a life; families being happy and families in trouble; travelling in time and staying in the moment, this volume brings you every kind of story told in every kind of way.

National Flash-Fiction Day Anthologies:

Ripening
(NFFD 2018)

This seventh annual instalment of the National Flash-Fiction Day (UK) anthology is overflowing with food-themed flashes. Authors include: Alison Powell, Angela Readman, Calum Kerr, FJ Morris, Ingrid Jendrzejewski, Kevlin Henney, KM Elkes, Meg Pokrass, Nuala O'Connor, Santino Prinzi, Tim Stevenson, TM Upchurch. The editors are Santino Prinzi and Alison Powell.

Sleep is a Beautiful Colour
(NFFD 2017)

Some of these stories will shock, others will amuse, but all will leave you wondering how intriguing life and the world around us really is. Authors include: Robert Shapard, Etgar Keret, Bobbie Ann Mason, Meg Pokrass, Tim Stevenson, Nuala Ní Chonchúir, Stuart Dybek, Santino Prinzi, Kevlin Henney, Pamela Painter, Angela Readman, Robert Scotellaro, Calum Kerr.

A Box of Stars Beneath the Bed
(NFFD 2016)

No theme, just great stories. Authors include: Sarah Hilary, Angela Readman, Claire Fuller, Paul McVeigh, Santino Prinzi, Nik Perring, Meg Pokrass, Michelle Elvy, Tim Stevenson, Debbie Young, Kevlin Henney, Nuala Ní Chonchúir and NFFD Director, Calum Kerr.

Landmarks
(NFFD 2015)

Geographical stories that take you places. Authors include: Sarah Hilary, Angela Readman, SJI Holliday, Nik Perring, Michelle Elvy, Tim Stevenson, Jonathan Pinnock, Nuala Ní Chonchúir and Calum Kerr.

Eating My Words
(NFFD 2014)

Stories of the senses. Authors include Michael Marshall Smith, Sarah Hillary, Angela Readman, Calum Kerr, Nuala Ní Chonchúir, Nik Perring, Nigel McLoughlin, Cathy Bryant, Tim Stevenson, Tania Hershman and Jon Pinnock.

Scraps
(NFFD 2013)

Stories inspired by other artworks. Authors include Jenn Ashworth, Cathy Bryant, Vanessa Gebbie, David Hartley, Kevlin Henney, Tania Hershman, Sarah Hilary, Holly Howitt, Calum Kerr, Emma J. Lannie, Stephen McGeagh, Jonathan Pinnock, Dan Powell, Tim Stevenson, and Alison Wells.

Jawbreakers
(NFFD 2012)

One-word titles only! Includes stories from Ian Rankin, Vanessa Gebbie, Jenn Ashworth, Tania Hershman, David Gaffney, Trevor Byrne, Jen Campbell, Jonathan Pinnock, Calum Kerr, Valerie O'Riordan and many more.

Printed in Great Britain
by Amazon